Graphic design and illustrations: Zapp
Story adaptation: Robyn Bryant

© 1994 Tormont Publications Inc.
   338 Saint Antoine St. East
   Montreal, Canada H2Y 1A3
   Tel. (514) 954-1441
   Fax (514) 954-5086
   www.tormont.com

   ISBN 2-89429-507-3

   Printed in China

RUMPELSTILTSKIN

TORMONT

There was once a miller who was very poor. All he had in the world was a beautiful daughter.

One day, the miller was called before the king because he had not paid his taxes. The miller had no money at all, so he told the king, "I have a daughter who can spin straw into gold."

"Bring her to me," the king said.

The king took the girl to a room filled with straw. "You must spin this straw into gold by morning, or you will be punished," he said. Then he locked the door.

The poor girl had no idea
how to spin straw into
gold. She threw herself
on the floor, and wept.

Suddenly, the door opened and an odd little man walked in. "Good evening, mistress miller. Why are you crying?" he asked.

"I'm supposed to spin this straw into gold, but I don't know how," she sobbed.

"**W**hat will you give me if I spin it for you?" the little man asked.

The girl gave him her necklace, and the little man sat down at the spinning wheel. By morning, all the straw had been spun into gold.

When the king saw the room full of gold, he became more greedy. He took the girl to a bigger room filled with even more straw, and ordered her to spin it into gold.

That night, the little man found the girl crying again. This time, he agreed to spin the straw into gold in return for her gold ring.

When the king saw so much gold, he became greedier still. He locked the girl in a huge room packed to the rafters with straw. "If you spin this into gold by morning, you will be my wife," he said.

That night, the little man returned. But the girl had nothing left to give him. "Then when you marry, you must give me your first child," he said.

The girl could not think of another solution, and agreed.

The next day, the king found to his pleasure that the huge room was filled with gold. As he had promised, he married the miller's daughter and made her queen.

A year later, the new queen had a baby daughter.

The queen forgot completely about the little man. But one day he appeared, and said, "Now you must give me what you promised."

The queen offered him all sorts of treasures if she could keep her child, but he refused. "Something alive is more important to me than all the riches in the world," he said.

At that, the queen burst into tears. Finally, the little man said, "I will give you three days to guess my name. If you succeed, you may keep the child."

The queen spent the whole night making a long list of all the names she had ever heard.

The next day, she read all the names to the little man, beginning with Abraham. But to each one, he replied, "No, that's not my name."

The following day, the queen sent out messengers all through the town.

"Bring me every name you can find," she told them.

The messengers brought back some very odd names, such as Ribsofbeef and Muttonchop. But to each one, the little man replied, "That's not my name."

By the third day, the queen was desperate. She sent out her messengers again to search the whole kingdom for any names they might have missed.

At nightfall, the last messenger returned with a strange tale. "As I was passing through the forest, I saw an odd little man dancing around a fire," he told the queen. "He was singing:

The queen will never win this game,
for Rumpelstiltskin is my name!"

That night, the queen asked the little man, "Is your name Alfalfa?"

"No, that's not my name," he said.

"Is your name Zebulon?" she asked.

"No, that's not my name," the little man replied.

"Could it be Rumpelstiltskin?" the queen asked at last.

When he heard this, the little man was so angry that his face turned blue, and he stamped his foot so hard that it broke right through the floor.

Then the little man disappeared into the hole and was never seen again.

After that, the king and queen and their little daughter lived happily ever after.